AF269517

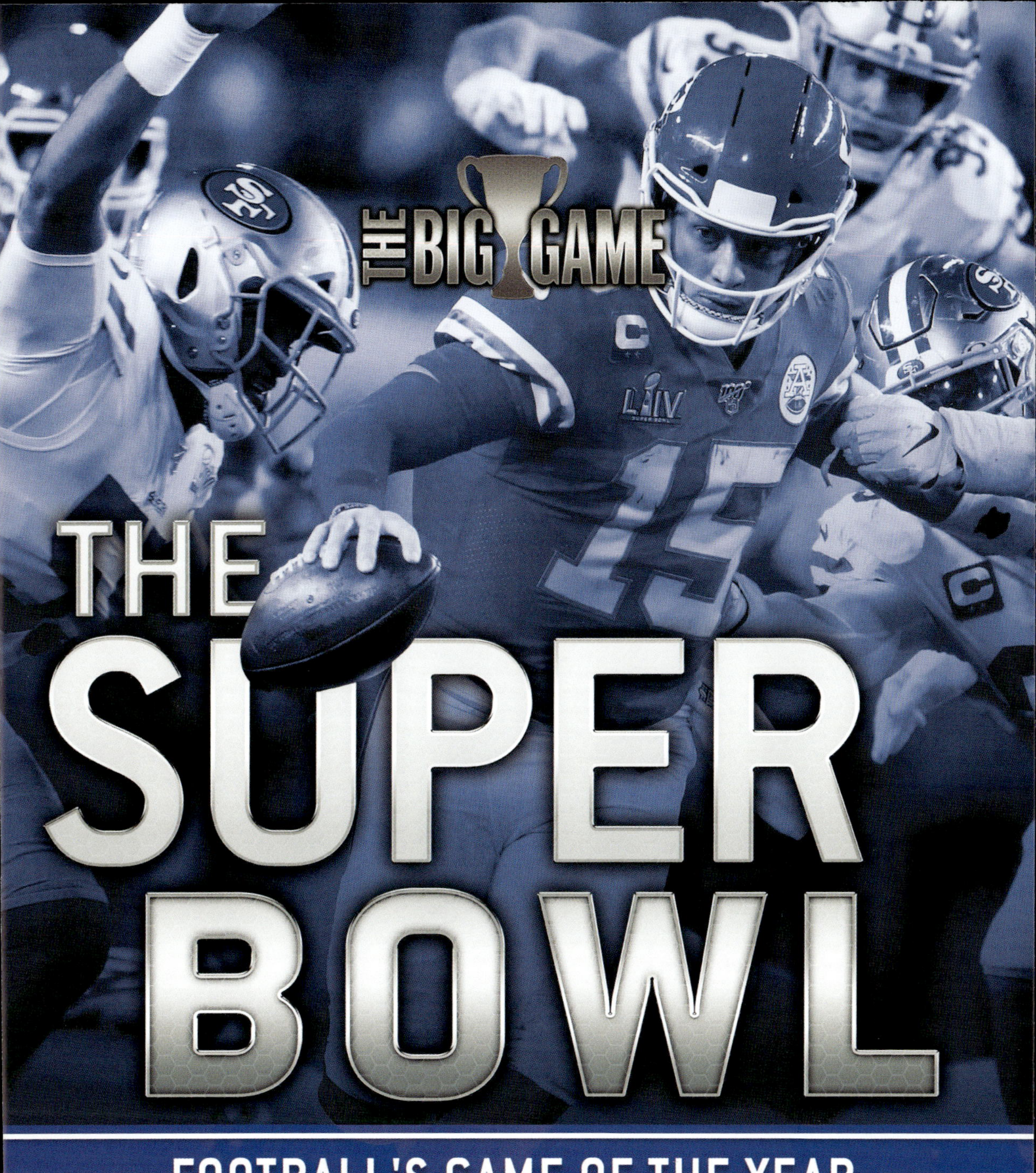

THE BIG GAME
THE
SUPER
BOWL
FOOTBALL'S GAME OF THE YEAR
Matt Scheff

Copyright © 2021 by Lerner Publishing Group, Inc.

All rights reserved. International copyright secured. No part of this book may be reproduced, stored in a retrieval system, or transmitted in any form or by any means—electronic, mechanical, photocopying, recording, or otherwise—without the prior written permission of Lerner Publishing Group, Inc., except for the inclusion of brief quotations in an acknowledged review.

Lerner Publications Company
An imprint of Lerner Publishing Group, Inc.
241 First Avenue North
Minneapolis, MN 55401 USA

For reading levels and more information, look up this title at www.lernerbooks.com.

Main body text set in Conduit ITC Std.
Typeface provided by International Typeface Corp.

Editor: Alison Lorenz **Designer:** Viet Chu

Library of Congress Cataloging-in-Publication Data

Names: Scheff, Matt, 1974– author.
Title: The Super Bowl : football's game of the year / Matt Scheff.
Description: Minneapolis : Lerner Publications, 2021 | Series: The big game (Lerner sports) | Includes bibliographical references and index. | Audience: Ages 7–11 | Audience: Grades 4–6 | Summary: "Explore the Super Bowl, the most popular sports event in the United States. Learn about the Super Bowl's history, its greatest moments, and the superstar players that make it the biggest event of the year"— Provided by publisher.
Identifiers: LCCN 2019044262 (print) | LCCN 2019044263 (ebook) | ISBN 9781541597556 (library binding) | ISBN 9781728401263 (ebook)
Subjects: LCSH: Super Bowl—Juvenile literature. | Football—United States—Juvenile literature. | Football players—United States—Juvenile literature.
Classification: LCC GV956.2.S8 .S34 2020 (print) | LCC GV956.2.S8 (ebook) | DDC 796.332/648—dc23

LC record available at https://lccn.loc.gov/2019044262
LC ebook record available at https://lccn.loc.gov/2019044263

Manufactured in the United States of America
2-53360-48299-5/13/2022

Contents

Comeback Magic

The 2020 Super Bowl wasn't going well for the Kansas City Chiefs. The San Francisco 49ers led 20–10 with just seven minutes to play. The 49ers defense had smothered Kansas City quarterback Patrick Mahomes all game.

Mahomes took the snap and dropped back. He hurled the ball down the field to wide receiver Tyreek Hill. Hill hauled it in for a 44-yard gain.

The big pass play changed the game. Mahomes threw a touchdown pass to tight end Travis Kelce. A few minutes later, he threw another touchdown to give Kansas City the lead. The Chiefs sealed the game with their third touchdown in five minutes. The team swarmed the field to celebrate their first championship in 50 years.

Facts at a Glance

- In 2017, after trailing the Atlanta Falcons by 25 points, the Patriots came back to win in overtime. It was the biggest comeback in Super Bowl history.

- In 2013, the lights went out at the Superdome in New Orleans, Louisiana, during the Super Bowl. It took 34 minutes to get them back on.

- About 98 million people tuned in to watch the Super Bowl in 2019.

- Quarterback Tom Brady has won a record six Super Bowls. Brady has been the game's Most Valuable Player (MVP) four times—another record.

CHAPTER 1

THE BIG GAME

THE NFL FORMED IN 1920. FOR DECADES, THE LEAGUE'S championship game crowned the best team in professional football. In the 1960s, the new American Football League (AFL) began to compete with the NFL. The leagues fought for the best players and the attention of fans. In 1966, the two leagues agreed to merge. Each league's champion met in a winner-take-all game, later called the Super Bowl.

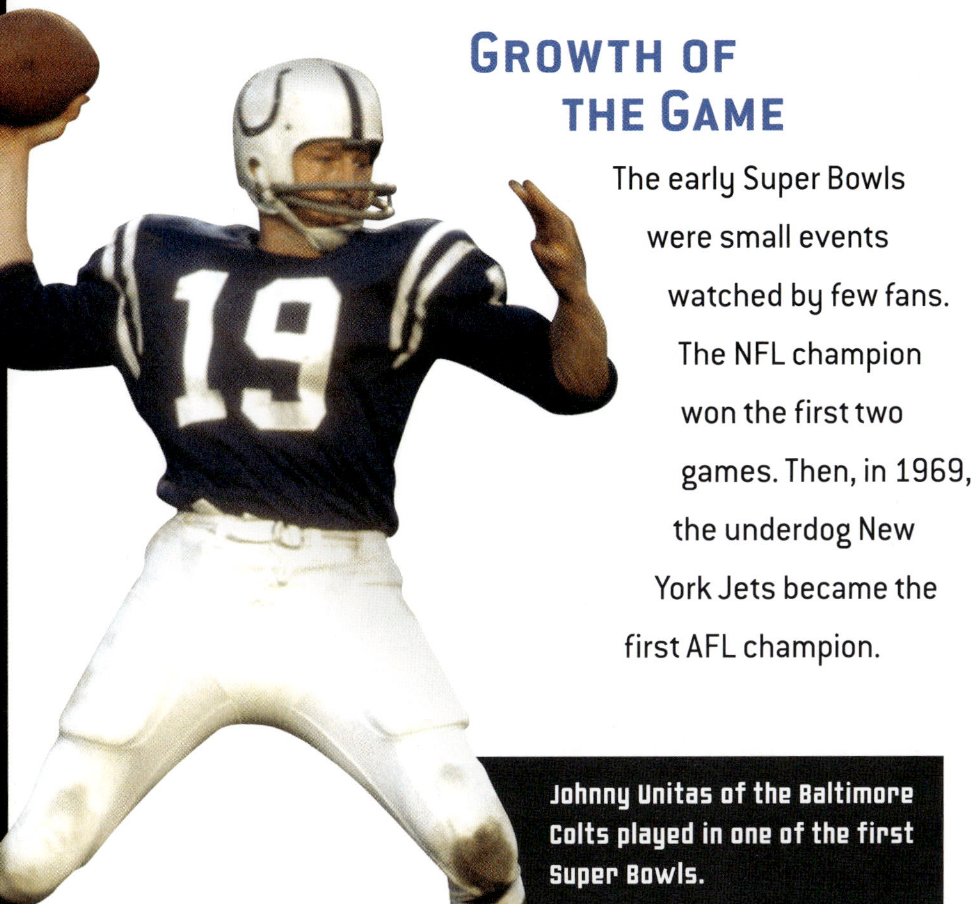

GROWTH OF THE GAME

The early Super Bowls were small events watched by few fans. The NFL champion won the first two games. Then, in 1969, the underdog New York Jets became the first AFL champion.

Johnny Unitas of the Baltimore Colts played in one of the first Super Bowls.

Inside the Game

Where did the name Super Bowl come from? According to legend, former Kansas City Chiefs owner Lamar Hunt first used the term. Hunt's children were playing with a toy called a super ball. That led him to blurt out the now famous name.

As fans saw the drama of the games, interest grew. Companies rushed to advertise during the game, and television coverage of the event improved. In the 1980s, the halftime performance became a major part of the show. The Super Bowl drew a worldwide audience, millions of fans, and billions of dollars.

President Barack Obama (*right*) and First Lady Michelle Obama (*center*) watch the Super Bowl in the White House theater in 2009.

Singer Lady Gaga puts on a
spectacular halftime show in 2017.

The Baltimore Colts, led by quarterback Johnny Unitas [*center*], were favored to win the 1969 Super Bowl.

CHAPTER 2

GREATEST MOMENTS

THE SUPER BOWL GIVES FANS THRILLS, CHILLS, AND drama. The 1969 Super Bowl set the scene for what was to come. Almost everyone expected the NFL champions, the Baltimore Colts, to crush the New York Jets of the AFL.

Before the game, New York quarterback Joe Namath guaranteed that the Jets would win. Namath led the Jets to a touchdown in the second quarter for a 7–0 lead. New York's defense did the rest. By the time the Colts finally scored, it was too late. The Jets won 16–7 in a huge upset.

Joe Namath of the New York Jets

The New England Patriots had been perfect all season. The team went 16–0 in the 2007–2008 season and cruised through the playoffs. Meanwhile, their Super Bowl opponents, the New York Giants, had barely made the playoffs.

Eli Manning of the New York Giants readies a pass during the 2008 Super Bowl.

The Helmet Catch was the last catch of David Tyree's career.

With less than three minutes to go, the Patriots led by just four points. Then New York quarterback Eli Manning led his offense on a drive for the ages. On third down, Manning took the snap, dropped back, and heaved the ball down the field. Wide receiver David Tyree leaped over a defender to reach the ball. Tyree pinned the ball against the top of his helmet. The amazing catch sealed a 32-yard completion. The Giants went on to score and win the game.

LIGHTS OUT

The 2013 Super Bowl saw the San Francisco 49ers face the Baltimore Ravens. After a touchdown early in the second half, the score was 28–6 Ravens. It seemed like lights out for San Francisco. Then the lights in the Superdome really did go out. Emergency generators kicked in, and players, fans, and the media waited in semidarkness until the lights came back on.

Shadows cover fans and players at the 2013 Super Bowl.

After the blackout, 49ers quarterback Colin Kaepernick nearly led his team to a comeback win.

The blackout delayed the game for 34 minutes. When the lights switched back on, it seemed to flip a switch on the 49ers too. In the final minutes, Baltimore clung to a 34–29 lead. San Francisco drove down to Baltimore's seven-yard line. But the 49ers couldn't get the ball into the end zone. The Ravens escaped with one of the strangest Super Bowl victories.

In 2017, the Atlanta Falcons had built a 28–3 lead over the Patriots by the third quarter. It should have been over. No team had ever come back from more than 10 points behind in the Super Bowl. Then quarterback Tom Brady led New England on one touchdown drive after another.

The Patriots' James White scores the touchdown that won his team the 2017 Super Bowl.

With three and a half minutes to go, Brady led his team on a grinding 10-play drive. After a touchdown pass to running back James White, White ran in the two-point conversion to tie the game. He scored again in overtime, completing the shocking comeback victory.

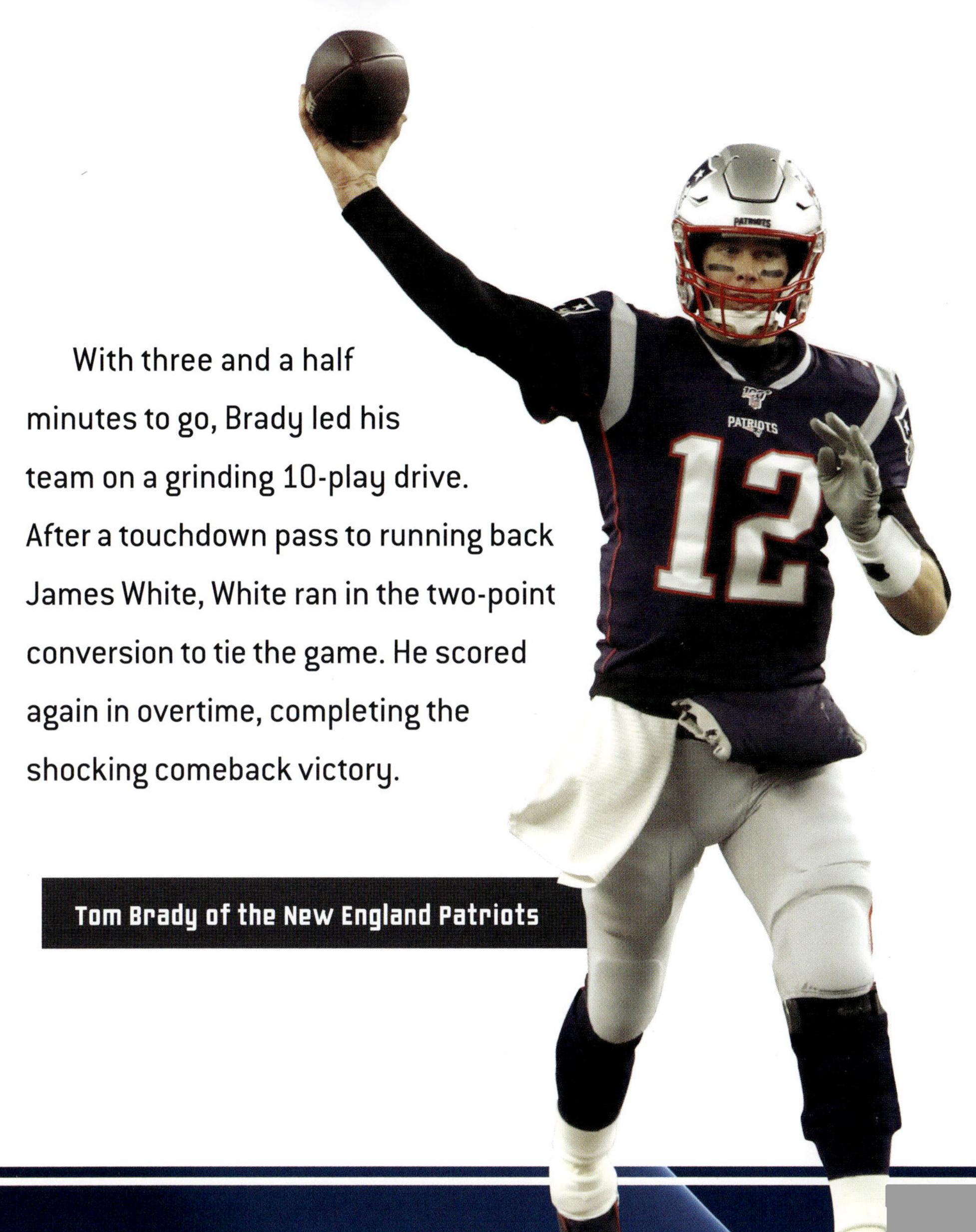

Tom Brady of the New England Patriots

Inside the Game

Do you love points? Then you would have loved the Super Bowl between the 49ers and San Diego Chargers in 1995. The teams scored 75 points together—the most ever in a Super Bowl!

Von Miller of the Denver Broncos reaches for the ball during the 2016 Super Bowl.

CHAPTER 3

CLUTCH PERFORMERS

FOOTBALL'S BRIGHTEST STARS SHINE ON THE NFL'S biggest stage. Quarterbacks make impossible throws. Running backs pull off incredible moves. Defenders shut down the opposition. Read on to learn more about some of the most clutch performers in Super Bowl history.

FRANCO HARRIS

Running back Franco Harris made his mark with a bruising running style. Many fans consider him the heart of the Steelers dynasty of the 1970s. Harris appeared in four Super Bowls with Pittsburgh. The Steelers won all four. Across the four games, Harris racked up a record 354 rushing yards.

JERRY RICE

Jerry Rice may have been the greatest wide receiver in NFL history. He always played his best in the Super Bowl. Rice won three championships with the 49ers. In the 1989 title game, he caught 11 passes for 215 yards and a touchdown. It was one of the greatest Super Bowl performances of all time.

TERRELL DAVIS

Running back Terrell (TD) Davis helped the Broncos win Super Bowl titles in 1998 and 1999. TD used a combination of speed and power to cut through defenses. In 1998, he was the Super Bowl MVP. He rushed for 157 yards and three touchdowns.

ADAM VINATIERI

No one beats Adam Vinatieri in clutch kicking. In 2002, he kicked a game-winning field goal for the Patriots as time expired. Vinatieri won three Super Bowls with the Patriots. Then he won one more with the Indianapolis Colts.

DWIGHT SMITH

Safety Dwight Smith played in the Super Bowl for the Tampa Bay Buccaneers in 2003. In the third quarter, Smith intercepted a pass and returned it for a touchdown. In the fourth quarter, he did it again. No other defensive player has scored twice in one Super Bowl.

VON MILLER

The Super Bowl MVP award usually goes to an offensive player. But in 2016, Denver Broncos linebacker Von Miller showed true defensive dominance. Miller racked up two and a half sacks and forced two fumbles in the Super Bowl. He helped the Broncos shut down the Carolina Panthers, and he won the MVP award.

ELI MANNING

New York Giants quarterback Eli Manning ruled his two Super Bowls. In 2008, Manning led the Giants to a stunning victory over the undefeated Patriots. Then, in 2012, Manning beat the Patriots again. He combined for 551 passing yards in the two games and won two MVP awards.

Tom Brady

No player has won more Super Bowls than New England quarterback Tom Brady. From 2001 to 2019, the quarterback led New England to an amazing nine Super Bowls, winning six of them. Brady earned Super Bowl MVP four times—another record.

Fans cheer on the Kansas City
Chiefs during the 2020 Super Bowl.

CHAPTER 4

Super Bowl Culture

THE SUPER BOWL IS THE NFL'S BIGGEST GAME. TENS of thousands of excited fans fill the stadium to watch. Millions more follow the action on television and social media. In 2020, nearly 100 million people tuned in to watch the Chiefs beat the 49ers.

GAME DAY

On game day, music acts and marching bands fill the air with sound. The players burst onto the field to huge applause. A singer—usually a pop or country star—comes out to sing the national anthem. Flags wave in the stands. Military jets soar overhead. Next comes the coin toss to determine which team gets the ball first. As the moment nears, the teams take the field for the opening kickoff. The game is on.

Inside the Game

Do you want to watch a Super Bowl in person? Start saving up. Super Bowl seats aren't cheap. In 2019, the average ticket went for more than $6,000!

At home, fans stay glued to their screens. They watch the game and laugh at the wild advertisements. Then comes the halftime show, filled with lights and music stars. When a team claims victory, the players, coaches, staff, and their families

Singers Shakira (*left*) and Jennifer Lopez perform at the 2020 Super Bowl.

The Chiefs' Travis Kelce holds the Vince Lombardi Trophy in 2020.

flood the field. Music blares as confetti rains down on the victors. The NFL commissioner presents the Vince Lombardi Trophy to the winning team. The game's MVP is honored while fans cheer.

Eventually, the stadium empties and the celebrations die out. The Super Bowl ends. Fans can't wait for football's big game to start all over again next year.

THE CHAMPIONS

Season	Winning Team	Season	Winning Team
1966–1967	Green Bay Packers	1983–1984	Los Angeles Raiders
1967–1968	Green Bay Packers	1984–1985	San Francisco 49ers
1968–1969	New York Jets	1985–1986	Chicago Bears
1969–1970	Kansas City Chiefs	1986–1987	New York Giants
1970–1971	Baltimore Colts	1987–1988	Washington Redskins
1971–1972	Dallas Cowboys	1988–1989	San Francisco 49ers
1972–1973	Miami Dolphins	1989–1990	San Francisco 49ers
1973–1974	Miami Dolphins	1990–1991	New York Giants
1974–1975	Pittsburgh Steelers	1991–1992	Washington Redskins
1975–1976	Pittsburgh Steelers	1992–1993	Dallas Cowboys
1976–1977	Oakland Raiders	1993–1994	Dallas Cowboys
1977–1978	Dallas Cowboys	1994–1995	San Francisco 49ers
1978–1979	Pittsburgh Steelers	1995–1996	Dallas Cowboys
1979–1980	Pittsburgh Steelers	1996–1997	Green Bay Packers
1980–1981	Oakland Raiders	1997–1998	Denver Broncos
1981–1982	San Francisco 49ers	1998–1999	Denver Broncos
1982–1983	Washington Redskins	1999–2000	St. Louis Rams

Season	Winning Team	Season	Winning Team
2000–2001	Baltimore Ravens	2010–2011	Green Bay Packers
2001–2002	New England Patriots	2011–2012	New York Giants
2002–2003	Tampa Bay Buccaneers	2012–2013	Baltimore Ravens
2003–2004	New England Patriots	2013–2014	Seattle Seahawks
2004–2005	New England Patriots	2014–2015	New England Patriots
2005–2006	Pittsburgh Steelers	2015–2016	Denver Broncos
2006–2007	Indianapolis Colts	2016–2017	New England Patriots
2007–2008	New York Giants	2017–2018	Philadelphia Eagles
2008–2009	Pittsburgh Steelers	2018–2019	New England Patriots
2009–2010	New Orleans Saints	2019–2020	Kansas City Chiefs

Glossary

clutch: performing at one's best in high-pressure situations

commissioner: the official who runs a league

drive: a series of offensive plays

dynasty: a long period of dominance by one team

merge: to combine two leagues into one league

professional: done as a paid job

sack: tackling the quarterback behind the line of scrimmage

snap: the backward pass or handoff of the ball at the start of a play

two-point conversion: a play, after a touchdown, in which a team tries to put the ball into the end zone for two more points

underdog: a team that is not expected to win

upset: a game or series in which an underdog wins

Further Information

Bowker, Paul. *Biggest Super Bowl Plays.* Mankato, MN: 12-Story Library, 2019.

Levit, Joe. *Football's G.O.A.T.: Jim Brown, Tom Brady, and More.* Minneapolis: Lerner Publications, 2021.

Morey, Allan. *The Super Bowl.* Minneapolis: Bellwether Media, 2019.

National Football League
http://nfl.com

Pro Football Reference
https://www.pro-football-reference.com/

Sports Illustrated Kids—Football
https://www.sikids.com/football

Index

Photo Acknowledgments

Image credits: Jill Toyoshiba/Kansas City Star/Tribune News Service/Getty Images, p. 4; Mtsaride/Shutterstock.com, p. 5; Focus on Sport/Getty Images, pp. 6, 7, 10, 11, 12, 15, 16, 20; Pete Souza/White House/Getty Images, p. 8; Valerie Macon/AFP/Getty Images, p. 9; Michael Appleton/NY Daily News Archive/Getty Images, p. 13; Ronald Martinez/Getty Images, p. 14; Elsa/Getty Images, p. 17; Thearon W. Henderson/Getty Images, p. 18; George Gojkovich/Getty Images, p. 19; John G. Mabanglo/AFP/Getty Images, p. 20; Bob Gevinski/Getty Images, p. 21; Doug Pensinger/Getty Images, p. 21; Peter G. Aiken/Getty Images, p. 22; Mike Stobe/Getty Images, p. 22; Andy Lyons/Getty Images, p. 23; Kyle Rivas/Getty Images, p. 24; Jamie Squire/Getty Images, p. 25; Tom Pennington/Getty Images, p. 26; Maddie Meyer/Getty Images, p. 27. Cover: Nhat V. Meyer/MediaNews Group/The Mercury News/Getty Images.